TOMMY NINER AND THE MOON OF DOOM

Kites

TAKE OFF WITH A KITE!

This lively series is designed for children who have developed reading fluency and enjoy reading complete books on their own.

The stories are attractively presented with plenty of illustrations which make them satisfying and fun! A perfect follow-on from the Read Alone series.

TONY BRADMAN

TOMMY NINER AND THE MOON OF DOOM

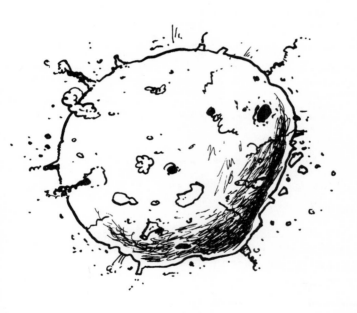

ILLUSTRATED BY MARTIN CHATTERTON

VIKING

VIKING

Published by the Penguin Group
Penguin Books Ltd, 27 Wrights Lane, London W8 5TZ, England
Penguin Books USA Inc., 375 Hudson Street, New York, New York 10014, USA
Penguin Books Australia Ltd, Ringwood, Victoria, Australia
Penguin Books Canada Ltd, 10 Alcorn Avenue, Toronto, Ontario, Canada M4V 3B2
Penguin Books (NZ) Ltd, 182–190 Wairau Road, Auckland 10, New Zealand

Penguin Books Ltd, Registered Offices: Harmondsworth, Middlesex, England

First published 1996
10 9 8 7 6 5 4 3 2 1

Typeset in 14/20 Palatino

Made and printed in Great Britain by Butler & Tanner Ltd, Frome and London

A CIP catalogue record for this book is available from the British Library

ISBN 0–670–86173–1

Contents

SPECIAL ORDERS

Tommy Niner sighed, chewed the end of his space pen, and tried to concentrate. He was alone in his cabin, doing the homework Dad had set him. It certainly wasn't Tommy's idea of fun. But there was no escape.

Commander Niner was a stickler for regular study periods. Today Tommy was supposed to be learning about landing and how to put your spaceship down on

11

the surface of any planet or moon, however dangerous.

The exercises weren't hard. They *were* work, though, and that was the problem. Work, work, work – it was all they ever seemed to do aboard the Stardust, thought Tommy. He was totally cheesed off with it.

His mind began to wander again. Soon he was lost in his favourite dream. They

were on holiday, and Tommy wouldn't have to work for weeks. He wondered wistfully if it would ever come true . . .

Suddenly the intercom buzzed, and Tommy jumped.

"Dad calling Thomas," said Commander Niner. "Do you read me? Over."

"Er . . . yes, Dad, I read you," said Tommy.

"Report to the control deck immediately, Thomas," said Dad briskly. "Something rather exciting has happened, and . . ."

"Great!" replied Tommy with relief. "I'm on my way, Dad!"

Tommy dashed from the cabin, his mind racing. What could the exciting thing be? Perhaps Dad was going to tell him Galactic Council HQ had given them some time off. Now that *would* be cool . . .

He reached the control deck door seconds later. Tommy hit the switch on the bulkhead beside it, the door hissed open, and he stepped through. Dad was sitting in his seat. Grandad was standing to the side.

"Ah, Thomas," said Dad, "I was just telling your grandfather we've had orders to make for Space Station Delta . . ."

"And pick somebody up," said Ada, the

Stardust's elderly computer. "It was one of those special scrambled messages, Tommy, and I insisted your father let *me* decode it. I adore puzzles."

"*As* I was saying . . ." Dad continued.

"Took you long enough though, didn't it?" muttered Grandad. "Call yourself a computer? I bet you have trouble adding up two and two."

"*If* you wouldn't mind . . ." said Dad, a little more loudly.

"Want to bet on that, micro-brain?" said Ada with an electronic snarl. "I could probably give you the answer in less than . . . twenty minutes!"

"Thundering thrusters," shouted Dad at

last. "I wish you'd all stop interrupting and allow me to finish. It's *very* important!"

"I'm listening, Dad," said Tommy. "Who is this . . . somebody?"

"None other than Admiral Kris Kelvin, Commander-in-Chief of the Space Fleet," said Dad, his eyes shining and his voice hushed with awe.

"Wow," said Tommy. "Where are we taking him?"

"Our task is simple, but absolutely vital," said Dad, putting a hand to his chest, and staring at the stars zipping past on the viewing screen. "We will be transporting Admiral Kelvin back to Galactic Council HQ."

"I think he means we're giving him a lift home," whispered Ada.

"It's my big chance," said Dad as if he were thinking aloud. "I might get a promotion, perhaps a brand-new ship . . ." A strange smile crept across his face. "No more putting up with crummy equipment . . ."

"That's you," Grandad whispered to Ada. She bleeped, indignantly.

"No more making do and mending," said Dad. Then his smile vanished, and his voice returned to its normal, grumpy tone. "So I don't want anyone messing up this mission. Is that clear?"

You'll be lucky, thought Tommy. But he didn't say a word . . .

② ENTER THE ADMIRAL

"So when is Admiral Kelvin expecting us to arrive, Commander Niner?" asked Ada. "I can't *wait* to meet him."

"In a couple of hours," said Dad, anxiously. "Crumbling comets, we'd better get cracking! I've made a list of essential chores, Thomas. I want this spaceship spick and span from tip to fins."

Tommy groaned as Dad proceeded to unroll a seemingly endless piece of paper. Dad was keeping most of the cleaning to himself, thank goodness, but there was still plenty of tidying for Tommy to do.

"OK, what have you got lined up for

me?" asked Grandad, rubbing his hands together. "I know, why don't I start by giving the engines the old Grandad once-over? Then I could . . ."

Dad ran a finger down his list while Grandad rattled on.

"Yes, here we are," said Dad after a couple of minutes, and a cascade of paper. "I knew I'd included you somewhere."

Item 164: Grandad - to be kept out of the way as much as possible.

"Charming!" said Grandad. "What are you implying?"

"That you're useless," said Ada. "Isn't it obvious?"

"Not to me, it isn't," replied Grandad. "I mean, we all have our faults, and I admit

I've had the odd spot of bother with some of the equipment . . ."

"Some of it?" said Ada. "You've wrecked nearly every machine on board!"

". . . And that I can be a bit absent-minded occasionally . . ."

"A *bit*?" said Ada. "Your mind's never even been present!"

". . . But there must be *something* I can do to help," Grandad whined. He fell to his knees in front of a stern-looking Dad. "Please? *Pretty* please?"

"Give him a break, Dad," Tommy said from the corner of his mouth. "You know how sulky he gets when he feels left out."

"Oh, very well," tutted Dad. "You're in charge of checking that the fuel tanks are full before we make our departure from the space station. Think you can manage that?" Grandad nodded eagerly. "Right, Ada," Dad said. "Full speed ahead!"

Tommy completed his chores and was on the control deck again an hour and a half later. It wasn't long before a small grey blob appeared at the edge of the viewing screen. Tommy knew what it was straight away.

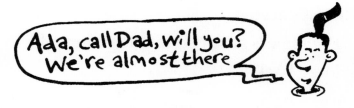

Ada, call Dad, will you? We're almost there

When Dad came through the door, the screen was completely filled by Space Station Delta. Tommy was fascinated to see the huge wheel turning slowly on its axis. Dozens of other ships busily whizzed round it.

Ada eased them into a docking bay and shut off the engines. Dad led Tommy and

Grandad to the Stardust's main airlock. "Crew . . . atten-TION!" he said smartly, and pressed the switch that raised the inner hatch.

Admiral Kris Kelvin marched through and saluted. He had shiny silver hair, steely blue eyes, a sharp, square jaw with a cleft in the middle, and so much gold braid on his uniform that Tommy was almost dazzled.

The Niners snapped to attention and saluted back.

Then Dad stepped forward. He opened his mouth – but no words came out! Tommy noticed he was shaking with nerves.

"What's wrong with you, man?" roared Admiral Kelvin. "Speak up!"

"W-w-welcome aboard, sir," said Commander Niner. "W-w-we're very honoured . . ."

"Cut the chat, Niner, and let's get going!" bellowed the Admiral. "You there," he shouted at Grandad. "Show me to my quarters!"

"But I have to . . ." said Grandad. The Admiral glared fiercely at him. "Aye, aye, SIR!" squeaked Grandad. "If you'd just follow me . . ."

Oh dear, thought Tommy. Suddenly he felt rather gloomy.

It looked like Admiral Kelvin wasn't exactly a bundle of laughs . . .

③ SHOCKING
Behaviour

Admiral Kelvin *hated* the guest cabin Dad had prepared for him. He said it wasn't what he wanted at all, and that it was vital he had a cabin with its own connection to the space radio. And he said it *very* loudly.

In fact, by the time they'd settled the Admiral in Dad's cabin and returned to the control deck, Tommy's ears were

ringing. He'd never heard anybody shout so much, not even Dad in one of his grumpiest moods.

"I'm *shocked*, I really am," said Ada. "If that's how high-ranking officers behave, I'm glad I don't have much to do with them."

"Hah!" said Dad. "I can see *you* don't know much about being a leader. The stresses and strains on the Admiral are probably enormous."

"He's certainly putting *me* under a lot of strain," moaned Grandad. "After a few minutes with him I wasn't even sure what day it was."

"That's not unusual," said Ada with an electronic giggle.

"Why, you . . ." Grandad started to splutter.

"Oh, stop it, you two!" said Tommy.

"Shouldn't we be leaving, Dad?"

"Quite right," replied Commander Niner. "The Admiral did say he was in a hurry. Thomas, I want you to fly us out of the docking bay. I'll set our course for GCHQ once we're clear of the space station."

"Actually, Commander," said Ada. "I think I'd better do it for you."

"Don't you *dare*," said Dad. "I'm giving the orders here, and I'll handle that job myself. You've made too many mistakes in the past."

"Can't say I blame you," Grandad said, and sniggered.

It was true, thought Tommy. Because of Ada, the Stardust often  ended up somewhere it shouldn't be. But setting a course *was* complicated, and

Tommy wondered if Dad was biting off more than he could chew.

You needed your wits about you to do course calculations. And the trouble over the cabins hadn't improved Commander Niner's nerves. Tommy thought he seemed in an even worse state than before.

"Suit yourself," said Ada snootily. "But you'll be sorry . . ."

Tommy sat in the pilot seat and fired the boosters. The Stardust rose and emerged from the docking bay. Tommy steered through the other ships and pointed the nose cone towards deep space.

"We're ready for that new course, Dad," he said.

"Be with you in a second," mumbled Commander Niner. He peered at the star charts spread in front of him, and tapped at his calculator. "There you are," he said at last, and passed Tommy the coordinates.

Tommy punched in the numbers, then turned on the main engines. The deck throbbed as they came to life, and the Stardust moved off.

Their mission had begun.

Dad called the Admiral over the intercom. "W-w-we'll be at GCHQ in three hours, Admiral Kelvin, sir," he said. "We've had no reports of meteorite showers blocking our route, so there shouldn't be any delays."

"Just let me know when we arrive, Niner," bellowed the Admiral, his voice

almost blowing the intercom out of the bulkhead. "And don't use the space radio during the journey. I have some urgent calls to make."

"Aye, aye, sir!" said Dad, sitting to attention and saluting. "Is there anything else I can do for you? I'd like you to know what I'm capable of."

But there was no reply. The Admiral wasn't listening, and Tommy could tell Dad was disappointed. It didn't matter, though.

Admiral Kelvin was about to discover what Dad was capable of anyway . . .

④ DAD'S DISASTER

For a while everything went smoothly.
The Stardust sped swiftly through space,
and Dad seemed to relax a little. Tommy
stayed at his post to help, but there wasn't
much that needed doing.

The clock ticked on monotonously. The
viewing screen showed nothing but
blackness, and the occasional star flashing
past. Then, after two hours and fifty-five
minutes, Dad pressed the intercom
switch.

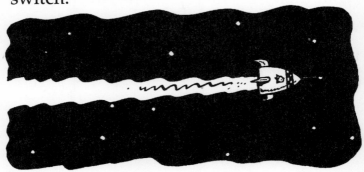

"Commander Niner calling Admiral Kelvin," he said.

"What is it, Niner?" roared the Admiral.

"J-j-just reporting as ordered, Admiral, sir," stuttered Dad. "We should be arriving at GCHQ in precisely . . . four minutes."

"About time too!" bellowed the Admiral. "I'm coming up."

"Aye, aye, Admiral," said Dad as the intercom went off with a squawk. Dad straightened his uniform, took a deep breath, and let it out. "OK, crew," he said firmly. "I want you on your best behaviour. The next few moments could be the turning-point of my entire career."

"I won't let you down, Commander," said Ada.

"Oh yeah?" said Grandad. "You always have done before . . ."

31

They started arguing, and Dad joined in, but it all washed over Tommy. He suddenly had the feeling that something terrible was going to happen.

The door hissed open, and everyone instantly went quiet.

Admiral Kelvin strode through and stood in the centre of the control deck, hands behind his back, his steely eyes fixed on the viewing screen.

Tommy thought he looked more bad-tempered than ever.

"S-s-so good of you to join us, Admiral," said Dad. "I hope you've had a pleasant trip. It's been a *great* privilege having you aboard."

Oh yes, I think we'd all agree with that

"Creep," muttered Grandad.

"Don't start, Grandad!" whispered Tommy. But luckily, Admiral Kelvin didn't seem to have heard, and Dad hadn't either. Tommy realized Dad's mind was totally focused on the Admiral.

"I w-wondered if I might have a brief word with you, Admiral," Dad was saying nervously. "I rather think I'm ready for promotion, and . . ."

"Is this screen working properly?" roared the Admiral.

"Er . . . absolutely, Admiral," replied Dad. "It's never worked better."

"Why isn't it showing GCHQ, then?"

the Admiral growled. "Precisely four minutes, you said . . . *and that was five minutes ago.*"

The Admiral was right. The screen still showed nothing but empty space. Tommy glanced at Dad, and saw the blood drain from his face.

"But . . . but . . ." stammered Dad. "It should be there . . ."

Well, it isn't, is it? What course did you set?

Dad pressed a switch. The Admiral glanced at the display, then seemed to swell to twice his size. "You blithering idiot, Niner!" he roared. "You've got it completely wrong! We're *thousands* of light years from GCHQ . . ."

"Eleven thousand, six hundred and seventy-three, actually"

chipped in Ada.

Tommy shot her a dirty look. "Just trying to be helpful," she said.

"I've never known such a nincompoop," the Admiral continued. "Promotion? Forget it, Niner. I'm going to make sure you and your useless crew spend the rest of your lives collecting space garbage. *If you ever get me back to GCHQ, that is! Now change that course!*"

"Aye, aye, *SIR!*" squeaked Dad, and the Admiral stormed out.

Then Tommy watched in horror . . . as his Dad burst into tears!

⑤ Mission Impossible...

Commander Niner slumped across the controls and sobbed like a baby. Tommy ran over, put an arm round his father's shoulders, and tried to calm him down. But Dad simply wouldn't be consoled.

"Holy solar systems, how could I have been that stupid?" he wailed. "I can't *believe* I made a mess of the course calculations! My career is deader than a burnt-out star. I'll be the biggest joke in the fleet!"

And he collapsed into floods of tears once more.

"I won't say I told you so," said Ada, but then she paused.

"Hang on a second," she continued. "This is too good an opportunity to miss. I *will* say it. I *did* tell you so. I remember it distinctly."

"Give it a rest, Ada," said Tommy. "Can't you see how upset he is?"

"*He's* upset?" said Grandad. "What about me? Didn't you hear what the Admiral has planned for us? I don't want to end *my* career collecting space garbage. I'm too old for that sort of dirty work."

"You're too old for anything," said Ada.

"Why, you miserable, pathetic pile of plastic and tin," Grandad replied furiously. "I'm still young enough to rearrange *your* circuits . . ."

Tommy sighed. What with Dad howling his heart out, and Grandad and Ada arguing with each other at the tops of their voices, his ears were beginning to ring again. Tommy realized *he* would have to take charge.

It was a tough job, but then *somebody* had to do it.

Tommy hit the red alert button. Immediately, warning sirens whooped, and alarm lights flashed on every instrument panel. Ada and Grandad shut

up, while Dad stopped crying and leapt to his feet.

"OK, now that I've got your attention," said Tommy, hitting the red alert button a second time to turn off the sirens and alarms, "perhaps we . . ."

"Am I correct in assuming you used the red alert button for no real reason, Thomas?" said Dad crossly, pulling a tissue from his pocket and dabbing at his eyes with it. "Regulations state it's only for emergencies."

"But this *is* an emergency, Dad," said Tommy. "We have to pull ourselves together and *do* something."

"Spoken like a true Niner," said Grandad, proudly. "You're a chip off the old space block, Tommy. It's just a shame most of my qualities seem to have skipped a generation," he finished, scowling at Dad.

"All right, point taken," said Dad. He blew his nose loudly before continuing. "But there's nothing we *can* do about it, is there?"

"Of course there is!" said Tommy, more confidently than he felt. "It's simple, Dad. We just have to show the Admiral he's wrong about you, and that we're the best crew in the Space Fleet. Then he'll change his mind."

"Sounds like mission impossible to me, Tommy," said Ada. Dad and Grandad were staring at him as if he'd gone bonkers.

"Oh, come on, you lot," said Tommy, determined not to be defeated. "Surely we can think of *some* way to impress him. Don't you have anything in your memory banks that might help us, Ada?"

"Well, there is something . . ." said Ada, reluctantly.

"What is it?" said Tommy, eagerly.

"I'm not sure I should tell you," said Ada. "And it's not from my memory banks, it's just a snippet of information I sort of . . . came across."

"Out with it, Ada," said Dad, sternly. "And that's an order!"

"There's no need to take that tone, Commander," said Ada, grumpily. "It's probably not even important. All I know is that the Admiral's daughter has run away from home. She's been missing for three days . . ."

6 A Mystery Revealed

"There you are," said Dad. "It's no wonder the Admiral has been rather . . . *difficult.* I knew the second I saw him he was under a great deal of stress. He must be worried sick, poor man."

"Have you got any details, Ada?" said Tommy, his interest aroused. "This might be more important than you thought."

"Really?" said Ada, brightly. "Well, as I understand it –"

Ada slipped into gossip mode, and revealed a fascinating story. She printed a picture of Kate Kelvin, who was the same age as Tommy. Kate had run away after a

severe telling-off from Admiral Kelvin.

She had stolen a small space shuttle from GCHQ, and nobody had seen her since, despite a galaxy-wide search. Of course, she might have gone into hiding somewhere. But she might also be lost, or in trouble.

Admiral Kelvin had visited several sectors to check on progress personally, ending his tour at Space Station Delta. But the searchers had drawn a blank there, too. Now time was running out.

The shuttle only had a limited air supply . . .

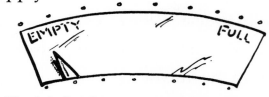

"So it's looking quite bleak for the Kelvins at the moment," finished Ada, cheerily. "What else would you like to know?"

"Just one thing, Ada," said Dad, sounding confused. "Why haven't we heard this piece of news before? Surely every ship in the fleet must have had a signal from GCHQ about it."

"I'll just check on that, Commander," said Ada. She whirred and hummed for a few seconds. "Er . . . whoops, silly me! Actually, we *did* get a signal, but I was asleep when it came in. I'm awfully sorry."

"So where did you get the information, then?" asked Dad, suspiciously.

"I'll bet she listened in to the Admiral's space-radio transmissions," said Grandad. "We all know she's the nosiest computer in the universe."

"What an outrageous suggestion!" replied Ada, angrily. "I, er . . . may have overheard some brief conversations between the Admiral and Mrs Kelvin,"

she spluttered. "But I would never deliberately . . ."

"Suffering sun-spots, Ada!" groaned Dad, slapping a palm to his forehead in despair. "The Admiral probably has us marked down already as very mean for not asking about his daughter. But I dread to think *what* he'll say if he discovers you eavesdropped on his private calls."

Ada tried to defend herself, while Grandad hooted with laughter. Tommy took no notice. He knew now what they had to do.

"He won't mind, Dad," said Tommy. "In fact, he'll think we're brilliant – *if* we find his daughter for him, that is."

"What a good idea, Tommy!" said Grandad.

"Hold on a minute," said Dad. "How

are we going to do that?"

"Leave it to me," said Tommy. "Er . . . I have a plan."

"You have?" said Dad, amazed. "Well, we ought to discuss it with the Admiral, then . . ." A look of fear appeared in Commander Niner's eyes. "On second thoughts, Thomas, as it's your plan, you'd better explain it to him yourself. Then you can tell the rest of us what he says."

"Now that's what I call a *really* good idea," said Grandad. "Cheerio, Tommy, and the best of luck. Don't forget, we're behind you!"

Yes, a long way behind me, thought Tommy, trudging off to speak to the Admiral. But that was OK. It meant he had a few minutes to do some thinking, without any of the usual distractions from his family.

For the truth was . . . Tommy didn't have a plan at all.

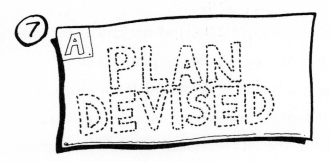

7 A PLAN DEVISED

Tommy stopped outside the Admiral's cabin and thought really hard. He *had* to work out a plan . . . but nothing came to him. The prospect of being shouted at by the Admiral had completely emptied his brain.

Tommy *loathed* being shouted at by adults, especially when he hadn't done anything wrong. Sometimes, if Dad was particularly unfair, Tommy felt like being as awkward as possible, just to get his own back.

Suddenly, Tommy had a thought. Maybe that's what had happened with Kate Kelvin! Perhaps *she'd* been told off for no good reason, and had stolen the space shuttle to spite her parents.

Tommy knew what *he would* do next in the same situation. He would head straight for anywhere Dad had expressly forbidden him to go!

It was a long shot, but it did give Tommy the makings of a plan – and he didn't have a lot to lose. Besides, Kate Kelvin's life could be at stake, and he knew he might just have come up with the key to saving her.

Tommy pressed the buzzer. The door hissed open.

"Yes?" roared the Admiral. "What do you want?"

"Permission to speak with you about your daughter, Admiral," said Tommy, saluting. "I have a theory which might help us find her."

"I'm surprised anybody on this ship

even knows she's gone missing," grunted the Admiral. "And what makes you think *you* can succeed where the rest of the Space Fleet has already failed?"

"Beg pardon, sir," said Tommy, "but they're adults. I'm a child, which means I've got a better idea of how Kate's mind works."

"Very well, I'll give you two minutes to explain this *theory*," bellowed the Admiral. "But if you're wasting my time . . ."

"I'm not, sir," said Tommy, crossing his fingers.

"We'll see," growled the Admiral.

Tommy stepped over the threshold, stood to attention, and started talking fast. He fired question after question at the Admiral, and the answers made him more and more confident he was on the right track.

The searchers had concentrated on places where *adults* thought Kate might have gone – friends' spaceships, planetary shopping malls, satellite burger bars. It just showed how dim grown-ups can be, thought Tommy.

"But you reckon Kate's gone somewhere we told her not to," mused the Admiral, stroking his chin. Tommy nodded. "I can think of three spots which fit *that* description," the Admiral continued. "Right!" he said decisively. "What are we waiting for? Let's check them out!"

Admiral Kelvin strode from the cabin, with Tommy following closely behind. On the control deck, Dad and Grandad leapt out of their seats and saluted. Ada started playing a little tune.

"What are you *doing*, Ada?" Tommy whispered.

"How else do you expect me to salute?" Ada whispered back.

"At ease, everybody!" bellowed the Admiral. "Young Niner here has suggested an interesting new approach in the search for my daughter. I am therefore temporarily taking command of this ship to test his theory."

Aye, aye, sir!

replied Dad, keenly.

"We will be checking three locations where my daughter might have gone," roared the Admiral. "The course for the first one is as follows . . ." The Admiral paused and punched the numbers into an instrument panel. "Computer, I want you to take us there immediately."

"But Admiral," said Ada, "that course leads directly to . . ."

"I know," growled the Admiral. *"The Spaceship Graveyard."*

Tommy gulped as he felt the Stardust change direction . . .

8 SPACESHIP GRAVEYARD

Tommy had heard plenty of stories about the Spaceship Graveyard. The tales were usually terrifying and featured ghostly crews, gruesome ghouls and awful alien apparitions.

It was the place where wrecks and abandoned vessels were brought so they wouldn't clutter the space routes and cause accidents. They were dumped in an area surrounded by asteroids at the edge of the galaxy.

The Stardust arrived there an hour later. As they approached, Tommy could make out the ring of asteroids, and hundreds of hulks hanging motionless inside it. Each ship was eerily dark and menacing.

This is definitely a *very* spooky spot, Tommy thought.

"I'm afraid my scanners aren't picking up any trace of your daughter, Admiral," said Ada. "Are you sure she might want to come here?"

"She was always saying she did," growled the Admiral. "Kate loves ghost stories, and wouldn't listen when I told

58

her they were all poppycock. Of course I couldn't allow her near the place. It's strictly off limits."

"Perhaps we ought to go in closer, Admiral," said Dad. "To be honest," he whispered, "Ada's scanners can be a little weak at times."

"I heard that!" snapped Ada, crossly. "And it's not true."

59

"It is," said Grandad. "Your scanners couldn't detect a planet if we were on the point of crashing into it. You're absolutely useless."

"Who are *you* calling useless, baldy?" crackled Ada.

"Er . . . I don't know about a planet," said Tommy, "but we're on the point of crashing into an asteroid unless we do something pretty quick."

While the others had been talking, the Stardust had flown steadily onwards, and an extremely large asteroid was dead ahead of them.

"Watch out, Ada!" yelled Dad. "You'd better take . . .."

"Evasive action?" said Ada. "I was just about to!"

Suddenly the Stardust lurched to one

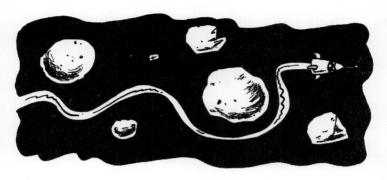

side. Tommy and the Admiral hung on
desperately to a bulkhead, but Dad and
Grandad were thrown from their seats as
Ada began to zig and zag crazily through
the asteroids.

At last they shot into the
space occupied by the
wrecks, clipping several and
sending them spinning end
over end. Ada fired the
retro-rockets and the Stardust screeched
to a halt, centimetres from another wreck.

"Phew, made it!" Ada chuckled
electronically as Tommy and the Admiral
relaxed, and Dad and Grandad staggered

to their feet. "Still, you did say we ought to go in closer, Commander. This is as close as you can get."

"Just tell me if there's any sign of my daughter!" roared the Admiral.

"Do you know, if there was a competition to find out who was the rudest man in the universe, nobody else would need to enter," muttered Ada. "I'll try my *pathetically* weak scanners." There was silence for a few seconds, then Ada spoke once more. "No, there's nothing."

"Blast!" said the Admiral, banging his fist down.

"Hey," said Tommy. "What's *that*?"

Now the Stardust was inside the ring of

asteroids, Tommy had noticed a hazy net of energy strung between them.

"I don't like the look of it," said Grandad.

"It could be a force field," said Dad.

"Top marks, Commander," said Ada. "That's exactly what it is."

"Well, what's it doing there?" roared Admiral Kelvin.

"I have no idea," said Ada. "And I wouldn't tell *you* if I had."

"I reckon it's a one-way force field," said Tommy, peering intently at the screen. "It lets the wrecks in, but not out again. Which means . . ."

"That we're stuck here, too!" the others yelled together . . .

⑨ CODE CRACKERS

They spent the next half hour trying to beat the force field. They charged it and bounced off a few times, then Dad and Grandad zapped it with the Stardust's lasers. But the hazy net still held them in.

"Staggering star clusters, Ada," said Dad. They were all feeling dizzy from the

collisions, and over-heated from the laser fire. "Can you find the generator? We'd have more chance if we concentrated on that."

"Actually, Commander," said Ada, "the generator is *inside* an asteroid, so it's well protected. It's also controlled by a very cheeky computer. He won't even speak to me. Apparently I don't know the proper access code."

Admiral Kelvin paced the control deck, growling impatiently. Tommy felt sorry for him. Time was ticking on, and being trapped here meant they were no nearer to solving the puzzle of where his daughter might be.

Tommy sat bolt upright in his seat. A puzzle, he thought . . .

"Listen, everybody," he shouted. "I know how we can get out of here!" Dad and Grandad stopped firing the lasers, and the Admiral turned to Tommy. "Ada, didn't

you say earlier that you adore *puzzles*?"
he went on.

"I did," said Ada. "Why do you ask,
Tommy?"

"Well, wouldn't working out the access
code for the force field computer be a
really interesting . . . puzzle?" said
Tommy. "I bet you could crack it!"

"I bet I could, too!" said Ada. "Just give
me a few minutes."

"A few years, more like," mumbled
Grandad. Tommy flashed him a look, and
he shut up. They waited . . .

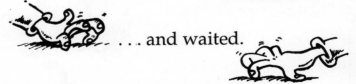

. . . and waited.

. . . and waited.

Then suddenly the force field
disappeared!

"Hurray!" yelled Tommy. "Terrific job,
Ada."

"Thank you, Tommy," replied Ada, proudly. "That computer was very sweet, really. Once I'd cracked the code he couldn't do enough to help. He even asked if I had a boyfriend," she giggled. "And *I* said . . ."

"Never mind all that!" roared the Admiral. "Our new course is . . ."

"So you don't want to hear the rest of the conversation?" said Ada, crossly. "Not even the bit about a certain runaway member of the Kelvin clan? Well, that's fine by me. I'll just rest my relays for a while."

"Of course we do, Ada!" said Tommy, glancing at the Admiral, who seemed to be holding his breath. "What have you found out?"

"Oh, not much," said Ada. "Just that your daughter *was* here, Admiral. The force-field computer said she turned up three days ago, and wanted to have a look at the wrecks. But he wouldn't let her, and she was *very* rude to him. I can't *imagine* who she takes after."

"Does he know where Kate is now?" asked the Admiral, breathing out with relief and excitement, and ignoring Ada's last remark.

"Not exactly," replied Ada. Admiral Kelvin sagged, visibly. "But he *did* say she flounced off in the direction of sector 17."

"That's just where I wanted to go next!" said the Admiral, perking up. "There's a place in sector 17 I've forbidden her to visit alone! Well done, young Niner. This is the first good news I've had for days."

Tommy smiled. He was relieved that his theory was working. But he couldn't stop worrying just yet. After all, they hadn't actually found Kate Kelvin, and the Admiral still didn't seem very impressed by Dad.

"Er . . . shall I g-give the order to leave, Admiral, sir?" Dad was saying nervously. "Or is that s-something you'd rather do yourself?"

"Just get on with it, man!" barked the Admiral, looking at Commander Niner as if he were some kind of repulsive alien life form.

Tommy realized he still had plenty to do . . .

10 ENGINE TROUBLE

Ada zagged and zigged out through the ring of asteroids, and soon the Stardust was speeding swiftly through space once more.

"Forgive me if I'm wrong, Admiral," said Ada, "but won't this new course you've set bring us rather near . . . *the Great Rift*?"

"I jolly well hope so," snapped the Admiral. "That's the place in sector 17 I meant. Kate's been interested in it for ages. She's been pestering me to let her go there, but it's a very dangerous spot."

The Admiral was dead right, Tommy thought. The Great Rift was notorious. It

was a giant, jagged rip in the fabric of
space, a kind of super black hole.
Anything that strayed too close was
sucked in.

"You're not kidding," said Ada as the
Stardust began to judder. "It's a long way
off, but we're already starting to feel its
pull."

"Perhaps we'd better check the area for
the Admiral's daughter as quickly as
possible," said Dad. "Then we can move
on."

"Good thinking, Dad!" said Tommy, but the Admiral didn't notice.

"Well?" he bellowed. "Any sign of her?"

"I'm afraid not, Admiral," said Ada. "Although I *am* picking up traces of spaceship exhaust. It's faint, but it might be from a shuttle . . ."

"That must be Kate!" yelled the Admiral.

"If it is," said Ada, "she was definitely making for the Rift. But she veered off in another direction about here. Very sensible of her, I must say."

The shaking was getting worse. Tommy glanced at the screen, and saw streams of space debris disappearing into a colossal cosmic chasm. Suddenly, the Stardust began making a strange, *hiccuping* noise.

"Any chance of changing course, Ada?" he said, nervously.

"Not at the moment, Tommy," said Ada. "We're having a bit of trouble with the engines. Perhaps it's because of this awful j-j-juddering."

"Don't worry!" yelled Grandad, dashing for the door. "I'll have them sorted out in a jiffy, or my name's not . . . not . . . oh, never mind!"

"Wait, Grandad!" said Tommy, racing after him. The last thing they needed was Grandad fiddling with the engines on his own! If he wrecked them, the Stardust was bound to be dragged into the Rift . . .

When Tommy arrived in the engine compartment, Grandad was hard at work with his space spanners. Sparks flew, and Tommy winced as Grandad happily clanged and banged away, whistling all the while.

Tommy put his brain into overdrive. He had to solve this problem before Grandad did any serious damage. He ran his eyes over the engines, and noticed a strange bulge in the power-transfer tube . . .

"I think I've found what's causing the trouble, Grandad," he said.

"Step aside, Tommy!" said Grandad. "I know just what to do!"

"Er . . . let's not be hasty now, Grandad," said Tommy, anxiously.

But it was too late. Grandad took aim at the blockage, then delivered a huge kick to the tube. Tommy couldn't bear to look. But it seemed to do the trick. The bulge instantly subsided, there was a loud

WHOOSH!

. . . and the engines finally stopped hiccuping.

Back on the control deck, Tommy thought he'd better make the most of their success. So he reported to Admiral Kelvin that they had managed to fix the engines – without revealing exactly *how*.

"Well done again, young Niner," growled the Admiral, sounding quite impressed, despite himself. "Right, let's get out of here."

"W-where to, Admiral, sir?" said Commander Niner.

Tommy's heart sunk when he heard their next destination.

"*The Moon of Doom*," growled the Admiral . . .

 Dangerous Descent

"Here we are, Admiral," said Ada two hours later. "Your daughter certainly picks some nasty spots to hang about in, doesn't she? I don't mind telling you, if we didn't have to save her, I wouldn't go near the place."

Neither would I, thought Tommy. They were in orbit round a large moon. It was covered in enormous volcanoes, most of which were belching billowing black smoke and rivers of glowing, red lava.

Tommy had seen pictures of the Moon of Doom. Now he was actually here, he understood how it had got the name. It was difficult to believe any living being could survive even a few moments on the surface.

But that's almost certainly where Kate Kelvin was.

After all, it was the third and last location the Admiral had forbidden Kate to visit. They had also tracked the exhaust emissions of a shuttle the whole way from the Great Rift. Then there was the distress beacon . . .

Ada had detected it as soon as she had started scanning the moon. It meant that Kate had either crashed, or landed and couldn't take off again. Whatever had happened, time was definitely running out for her – fast.

"Why are we waiting?" roared the Admiral. "We've pinpointed the distress-beacon's position, so let's hurry up and rescue her!"

"Don't look at me," said Ada. "If you think *I'm* taking us down there, you've got another think coming. It's been a long day, and I'm just not up to any fancy flying. I'd love to help, but . . ."

"Flaming fireballs, Ada!" said Dad, crossly. The Admiral was spluttering furiously, and his face had gone as red as the lava.

"It's OK, Dad," said Tommy. "I'll do it. Ada, give me manual steering."

"I'll be happy to," said Ada.

"Just a second, Thomas," said Dad, nervously. "Are you sure . . ."

"Oh, stop fussing," said Grandad. "When I was his age I was landing spaceships in far worse places every day. Go for it, Tommy!"

"Prepare for descent, everybody!" said Tommy, sitting in the pilot seat and gripping the controls. He fired the thrusters, and the Stardust zoomed towards the volcanoes beneath. "Hang on

to your false teeth, Grandad!"

It was a dangerous, scary ride. The
smoke made it difficult to see where they
were going, and they had to dodge huge
boulders blown into their flight path.
Tommy was glad he'd done the
homework Dad had set earlier.

Tommy took them as low as he dared,
skimming the surface and its vast,
bubbling seas of boiling lava. They
snaked between the volcanoes, and then,
suddenly, Tommy saw something in the
distance.

"There she is!" he shouted.

Tommy landed next to a shuttle on a tiny island of solid ground. The shuttle had obviously crashed, but standing beside it was the small, space-suited, and frantically waving figure of . . . Kate Kelvin!

"Quick, let's pick her up!" yelled the Admiral.

"Aye, aye, sir!" said Dad, and raced off with Grandad to the main airlock. Seconds later the intercom on the control-deck buzzed. "Dad calling Thomas . . . we've got her. You can take off now, over."

Tommy didn't reply. He simply hit the switch to fire the boosters . . .

But nothing happened!

"What's wrong, Ada?" he said.

"Why aren't we moving?"

"Oh, that's because we've run out of fuel," she said, cheerily.

"*WHAT?!*" yelled Tommy, horrified.

"And that's not our only problem, Tommy," said Ada. "I've been doing a bit of checking and I've discovered the whole moon is pretty unstable. In fact, I think it's going to explode . . . *at any moment!*"

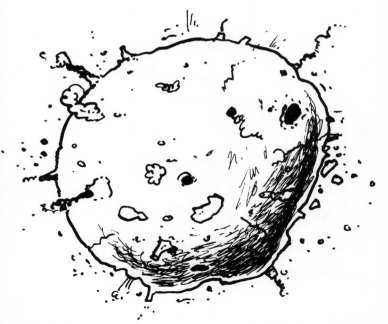

The Big Bang

Just then the control-deck doors opened, and Dad and Grandad arrived with Kate Kelvin. She ran over to the Admiral, and hugged him.

"I'm sorry, Daddy," she said. "I know I shouldn't have run off, and I promise I won't ever do it again. Cross my heart! I've been so scared . . ."

"I'm feeling a trifle nervous myself," said Commander Niner. "That lava's pretty powerful stuff. It's giving off an awful lot of energy. Now, would anyone care to tell me why we're still here?"

Tommy explained the situation . . . and everyone started arguing.

"I thought I told you to make certain the fuel tanks were full before we left Space Station Delta, you old twit!" Dad yelled at Grandad.

"I was going to," said Grandad. "But *he* made me show him to his quarters instead," he added, pointing at the Admiral, "so I couldn't."

"This is all *your* fault then, you high-ranking bully!" said Ada.

"*My* fault?" roared the Admiral. "How dare you . . ."

Tommy sat there, sunk in deep gloom, waiting for the big bang that would put him out of his misery. He'd got so close, too. He'd found Kate Kelvin, and solved each problem . . . except the last one.

But then he had a thought. What had
Dad said? The lava was *giving off an awful
lot of energy* . . . maybe this problem was
part of the answer!

"*QUIET!*" shouted Tommy, interrupting
the row. "Ada, could we use some of the
lava as fuel? I mean, would it work with
our engines?"

"Your guess is as good as mine," said

Ada. "It's worth a try, though."

"All hands outside to load lava in the fuel tanks!" said Tommy.

"I'll fetch some buckets," said Dad. "And my rubber gloves . . ."

The next few minutes were a blur of activity. They formed a human chain as the Moon of Doom rumbled beneath their feet. When the tanks were full, they

climbed back in the Stardust and
slammed the door.

"OK, Ada," said Tommy. "Start the
countdown!"

"Five . . .

    four . . .

        three . . .

            two . . .

                one . . .

                    ignition . . ."

Tommy fired the boosters. Nothing
happened. Tommy gulped, and tried
again. The boosters coughed a couple of
times . . . but then the Stardust started to
rise at terrific speed. "I think you could
say we have lift-off," Ada added.

Just as well, thought Tommy. For no
sooner had they escaped from the Moon
of Doom . . . than it exploded with a huge
BANG! The Stardust was rocked from
side to side as burning boulders flew past.

Tommy gripped the controls. He moved the Stardust this way and that, and then suddenly . . . they hit clear space again. They were safe!

"You were great, Tommy," said Grandad.

"Yes, Thomas," said Dad, putting his arm round Tommy's shoulders.

"Heaven knows how we would have managed without you."

"I couldn't agree more," growled Admiral Kelvin. "Now, atten-TION, crew of the Stardust. I have something very important to say." The Niners snapped to attention, and Ada played her little tune. "I think I owe you an apology. Despite everything, you *did* save my daughter."

90

"Yes, thanks *very* much!" said Kate.

"So you can forget what I said about collecting space garbage," growled the Admiral. Tommy breathed a sigh of relief. "Although you *do* need to pull your space socks up. Apart from young Niner, of course."

"Don't worry, sir," said Dad eagerly. "We'll try *much* harder!"

"I'm glad to hear it," snorted the Admiral. Then Kate nudged him. "Oh yes, and is there anything I can do to show you my gratitude?"

"Actually, there is," said Tommy, smiling. "Some time off would be nice . . ."

Who said that dreams never come true?